Disney • PIXAR

TOY STORY

Coloring Book

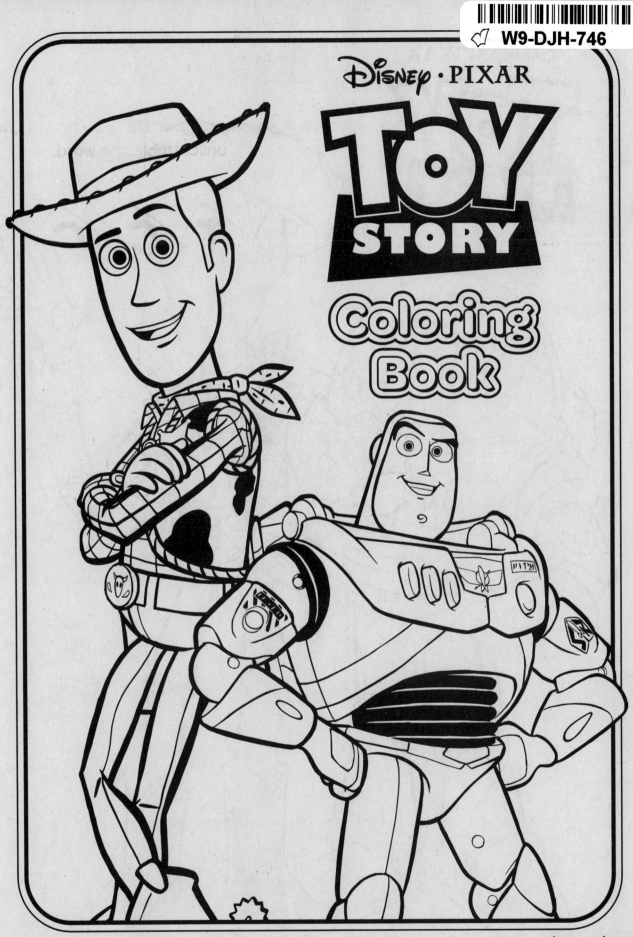

bendon

The BENDON name, logo, and Tear and Share are
trademarks of Bendon, Inc. Ashland, OH 44805.

Woody loves to play with Andy.

Woody has a special spot on Andy's bed.

SQUARES

Taking turns, connect a line from one sheriff star to another. Whoever makes the line that completes the box puts his or her initial in the box. The person with the most squares at the end of the game wins!

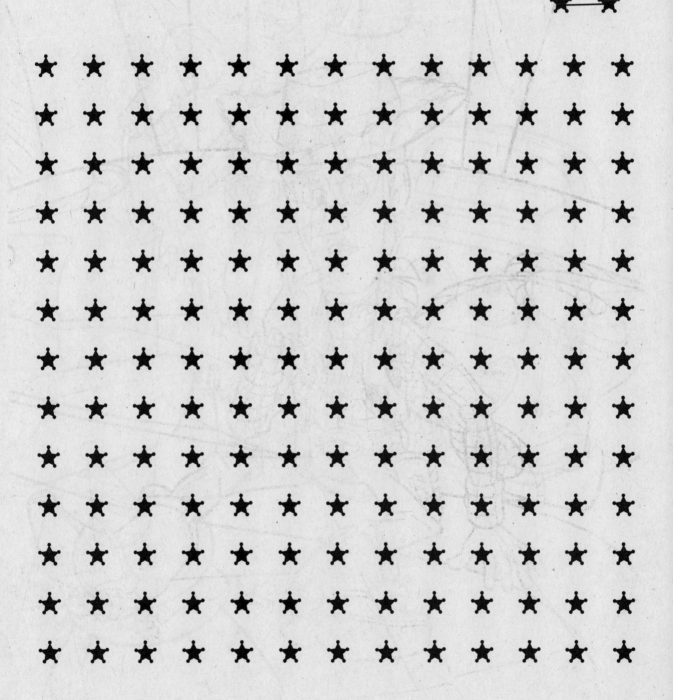

The other toys listen to Woody.

Help Mr. & Mrs. Potato Head get through the maze.

Rex is a lovable dinosaur!

Disney · PIXAR

TOY STORY

PUZZLE

© Disney/Pixar

MATCHING

Which two images are exactly the same?

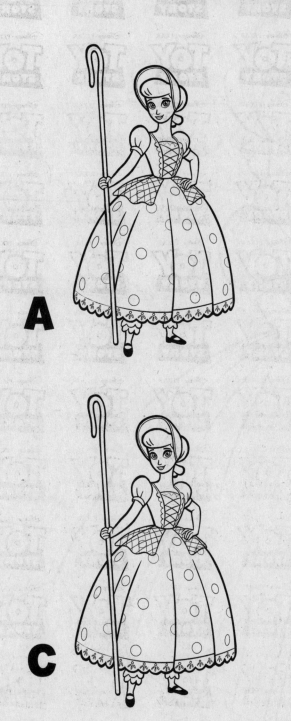

A

B

C

D

Bo Peep is a very caring toy.

UNSCRAMBLE

Unscramble the names listed below.

ODOYW

_ _ _ _ _

ANSWERS: Woody

KLNSIY

_ _ _ _ _ _

ANSWERS: Slinky

ZUBZ

_ _ _ _

ANSWERS: Buzz

RGSAE

_ _ _ _ _

ANSWERS: Sarge

© Disney/Pixar

Slinky Dog can stretch!

WHICH PATH LEADS MR. POTATO HEAD TO MRS. POTATO HEAD?

Hamm protects Andy's coins.

Happy birthday, Andy!

DRAW ANDY!

Follow the top grid to draw Andy.

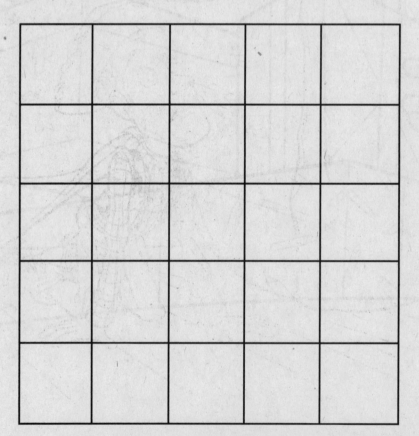

Woody is eager to meet Andy's new toy.

Buzz Lightyear is a space ranger.

SECRET MESSAGE

Cross out the word RANGER every time
you see it in the box. When you reach a letter
that does not belong, write it in the circles below
to reveal the secret message.

```
R A N G E R M R A N G E R
I R A N G E R R A N G E R S
R A N G E R S R A N G E R
I R A N G E R O R A N G E R N
R A N G E R T R A N G E
R O R A N G E R Y R A N G E
R R R A N G E R E R A N
G E R R A N G E R S R A N
G E R C R A N G E R R A N G
E R U R A N G E R E R A N G E R
```

◯ ◯ ◯ ◯ ◯ ◯ ◯

◯ ◯ ◯   ◯ ◯ ◯ ◯ ◯ ◯

To infinity . . . and beyond!

SQUARES

Taking turns, connect a line from one sheriff star to another.
Whoever makes the line that completes the box puts his or her
initial in the box. The person with the most squares
at the end of the game wins!

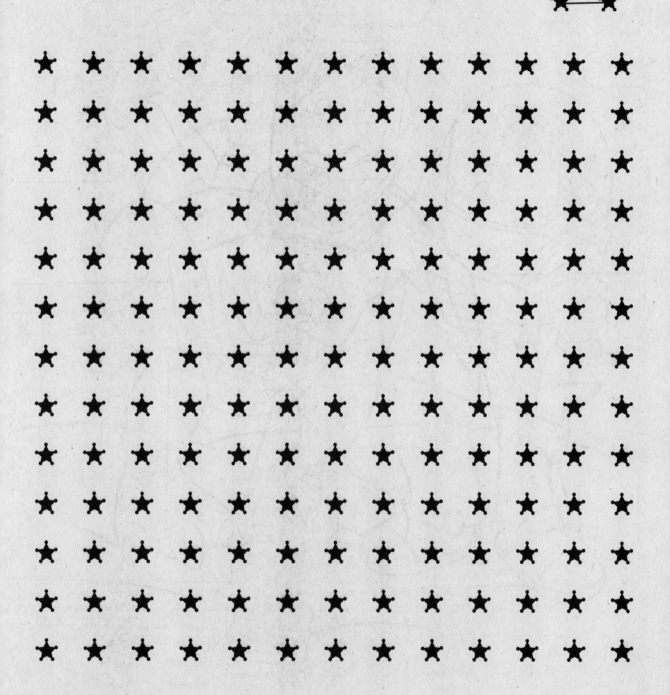

Buzz and Rex get along well together.

MATCHING

Which two images are exactly the same?

A

B

C

D

Uh-oh! Buzz takes a fall.

HOW MANY?

How many aliens do you see?

ANSWER:

ANSWER: 6

Hold on tight, Buzz!

DRAW BUZZ!

Follow the top grid to draw Buzz Lightyear.

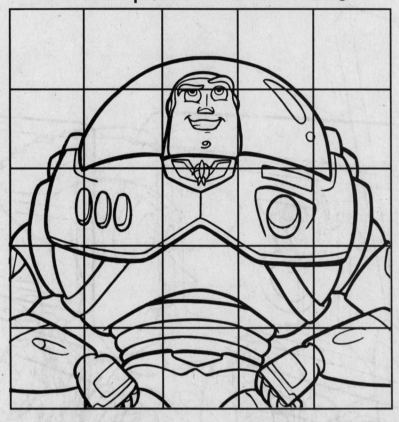

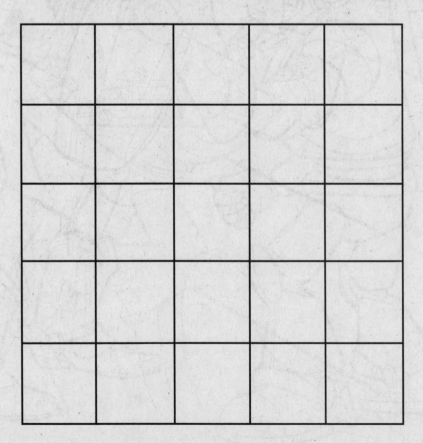

Woody is *not* happy with Buzz.

WHICH PATH LEADS REX TO HAMM?

© Disney/Pixar

Buzz and Woody put on clever costumes.

INTERLOCK

Using the words from the list, complete
this interlocked word puzzle.

SPACESHIP

GALAXY   ALIENS

LASER   INFINITY

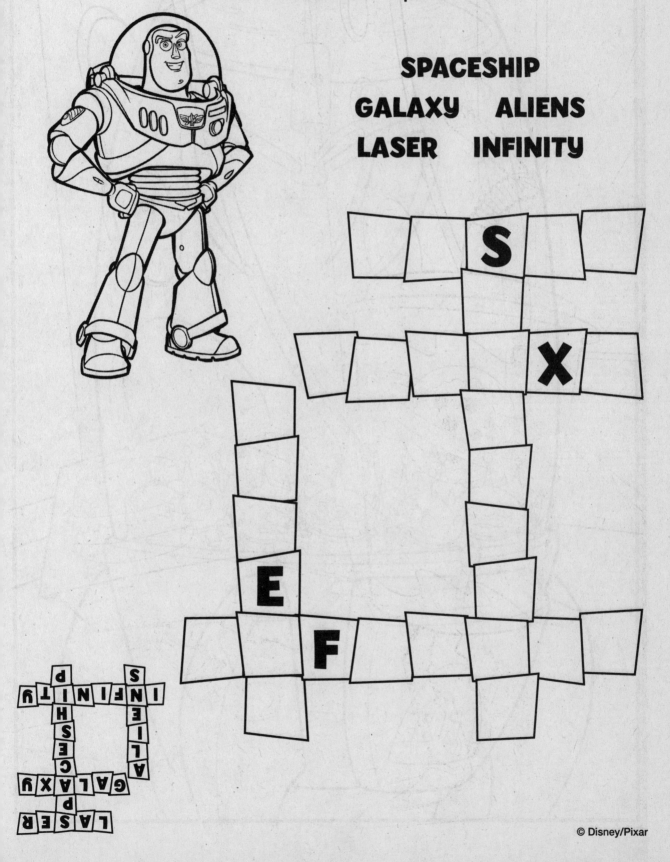

Toy Aliens are prizes in the Rocket Ship Crane Game.

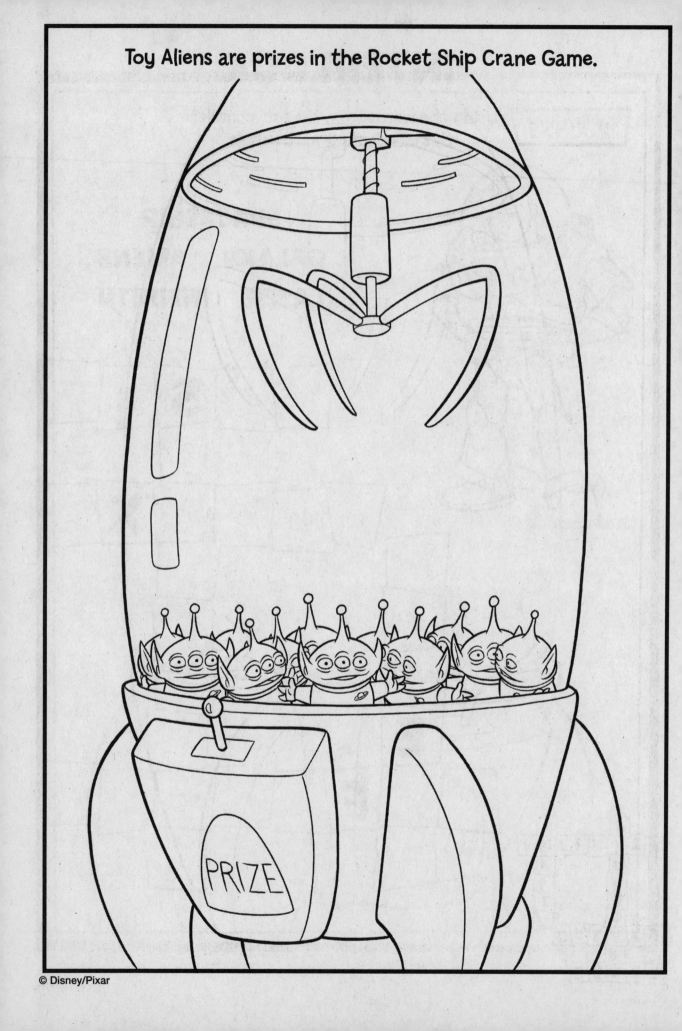

PRIZE

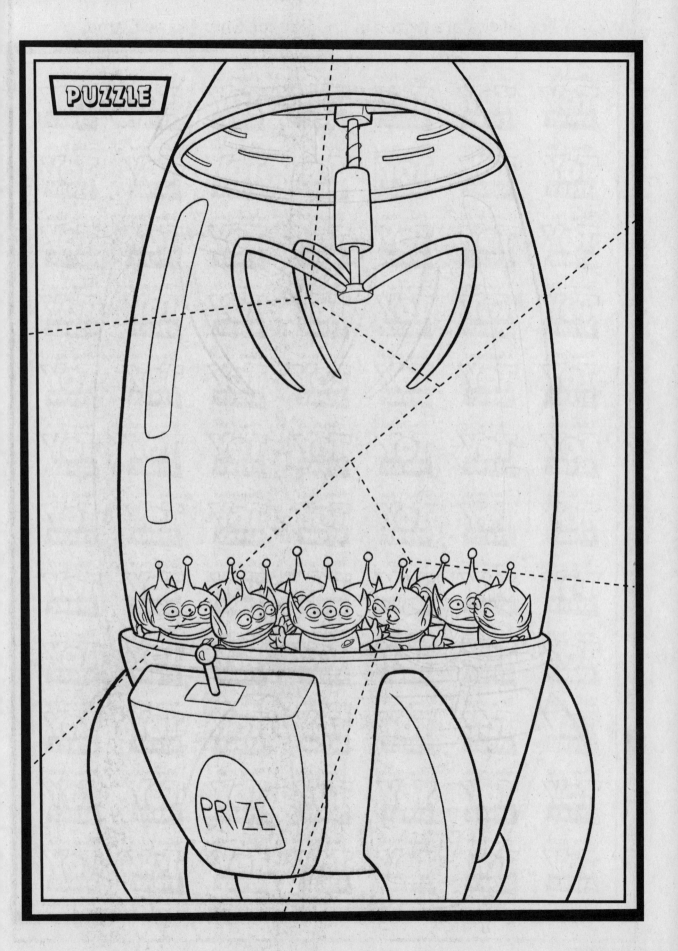

PUZZLE

© Disney/Pixar

The Claw has chosen Buzz and Woody!

TIC-TAC-TOE

Use these tic-tac-toe grids to
challenge your family and friends!

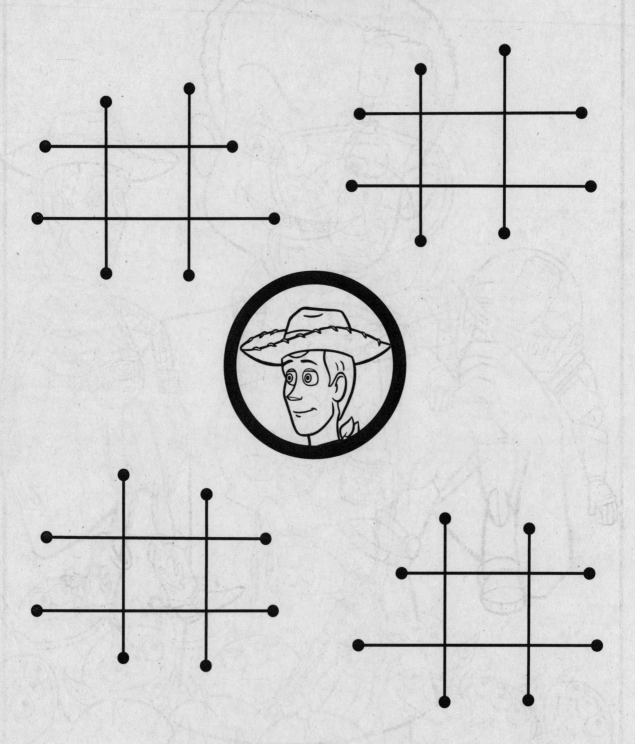

Sid is Andy's mean neighbor!

Help the aliens get through the maze.

TIC-TAC-TOE

Use these tic-tac-toe grids to
challenge your family and friends!

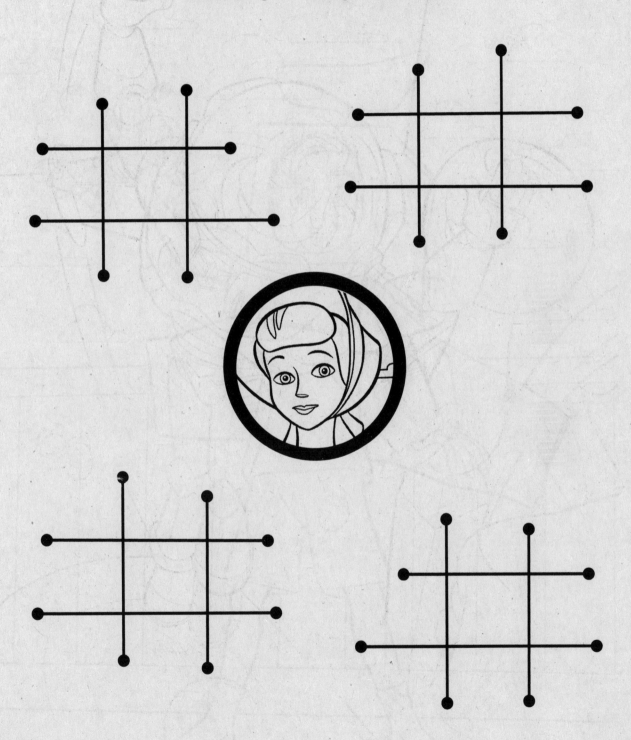

Andy wants to be a space ranger, too.

Buzz and Woody back away from Sid's mutant toys.

TOY STORY

WORD LIST

- ☐ **WOODY**
- ☐ **BO PEEP**
- ☐ **HAMM**

- ☐ **BUZZ**
- ☐ **REX**
- ☐ **SCUD**
- ☐ **SID**
- ☐ **ANDY**

Disney · PIXAR
TOY STORY
WORD SEARCH

O B A N D Z T Q
T U X W Y R E X
G Z V O E Z I H
X Z B O P E E P
H H J D V N A O
A N D Y B W S Z
M S P Q A N I R
M D Y S C U D M

SQUARES

Taking turns, connect a line from one sheriff star to another.
Whoever makes the line that completes the box puts his or her
initial in the box. The person with the most squares
at the end of the game wins!

Sid is eager to use his new rocket—on Buzz!

TRANSFER

Using the paths, transfer the letters into the boxes to unscramble the word.

L I T G C A A

ANSWER: GALACTIC

SQUARES

Taking turns, connect a line from one star to another.
Whoever makes the line that completes the box puts his or her
initial in the box. The person with the most squares
at the end of the game wins!

K

Andy's toys gather around his TV.

ZURG

BUZZ

DRAW HAMM!

Follow the top grid to draw Hamm.

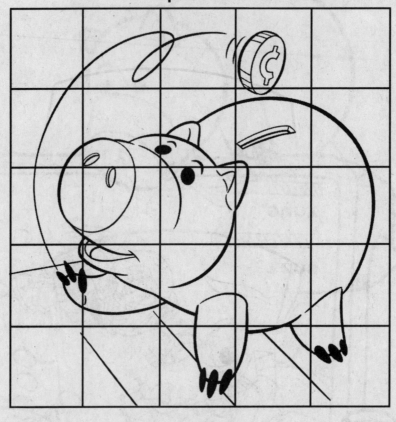

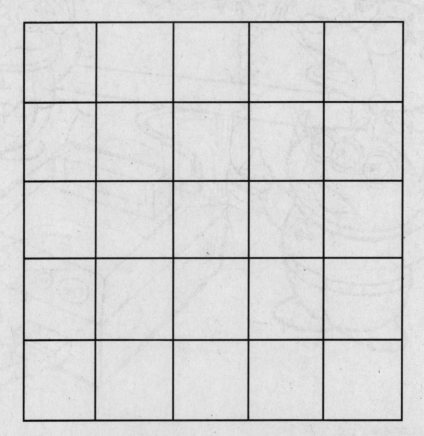

Andy has fun playing with his toys.

WHICH PATH LEADS THE ALIEN TO HIS FRIENDS?

Woody meets the Roundup gang!

YEE HAW

Bullseye needs some new shoes!
Color all of the small horseshoes.

The Prospector greets Woody.

Help Jesse get through the maze.

The Cleaner goes to work on Woody.

WHICH PATH LEADS WOODY TO JESSE?

A B C

ANSWER: C

© Disney/Pixar

Jessie is very sad.

DRAW SLINKY DOG!

Follow the top grid to draw Slinky Dog.

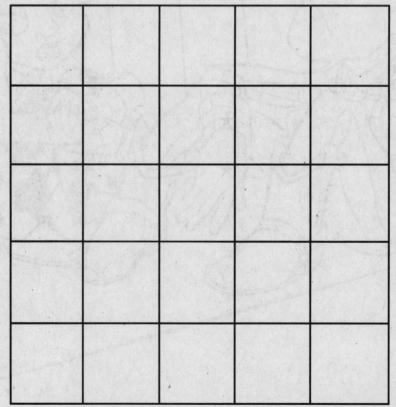

SQUARES

Taking turns, connect a line from one star to another.
Whoever makes the line that completes the box puts his or her
initial in the box. The person with the most squares
at the end of the game wins!

K

Jessie's owner gave her away many years ago.

Al's Toy Barn is a big toy store.

DOT-TO-DOT

Connect the dots to complete the image of the alien.

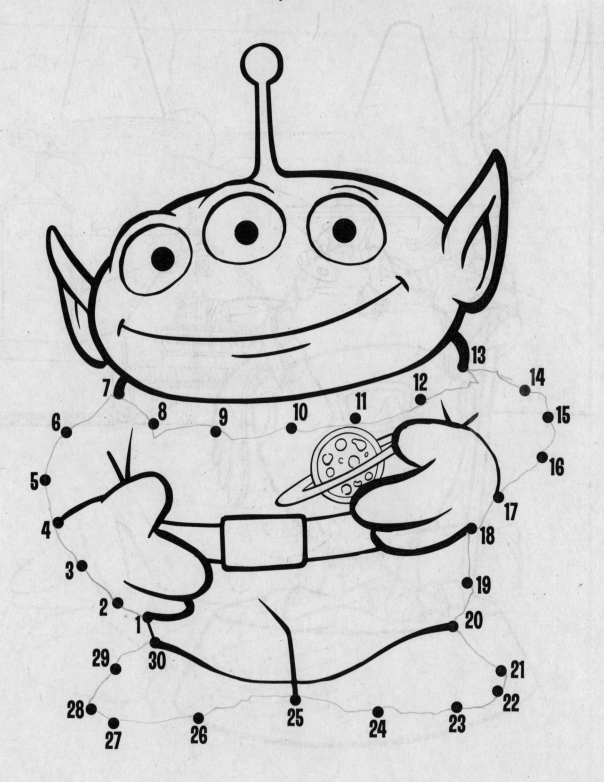

Buzz won't let Al get away without a chase.

COIN COLLECTOR

Hamm's an expert at saving!
Help him by coloring all of the large coins.

Buzz leads the way.

Help Buzz and the gang get through the maze.

Hamm and Rex explore Al's Toy Barn.

PUZZLE

How many aliens do you see?

Rex prepares to defeat Emperor Zurg!

TEAM AWESOME

Draw a picture of yourself as a toy!

Disney • PIXAR
TOY STORY

WORD LIST

☐ **BOOTS**   ☐ **BANDANA**

☐ **SPUR**   ☐ **SADDLE**

☐ **SHERIFF**   ☐ **CACTUS**

☐ **HORSE**

☐ **BADGE**

TOY STORY

WORD SEARCH

J K B A D G E E
V I A R Y L H D
H C N C T U O B
S A D D L E R O
S C A Q S P S O
W T N B P M E T
G U A N U A F S
O S H E R I F F

The toys cruise the aisles.

WHICH PATH LEADS BULLSEYE TO JESSE?

A B C

It's a brand-new Buzz Lightyear!

DOT-TO-DOT

Connect the dots to complete the image of Hamm.

Buzz meets . . . himself!

TIC-TAC-TOE

Use these tic-tac-toe grids to
challenge your family and friends!

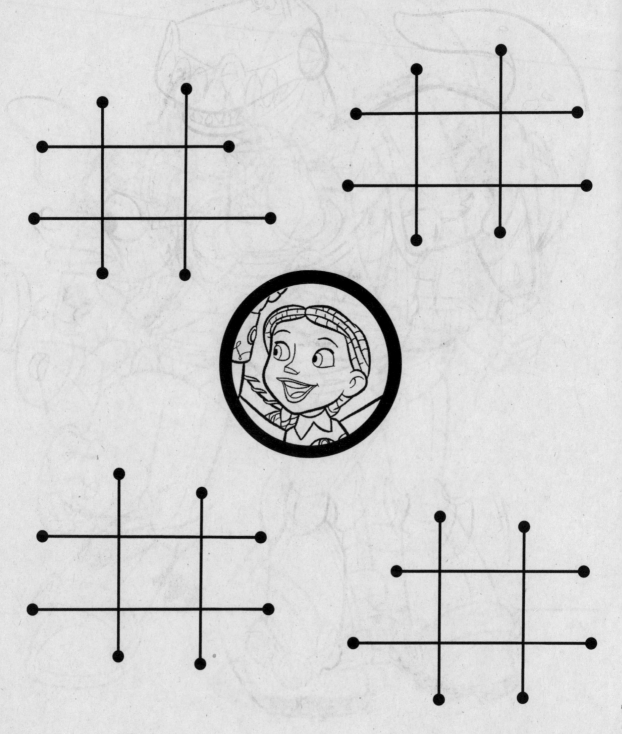

The toys have to hurry!

How many sheriff badges do you see?

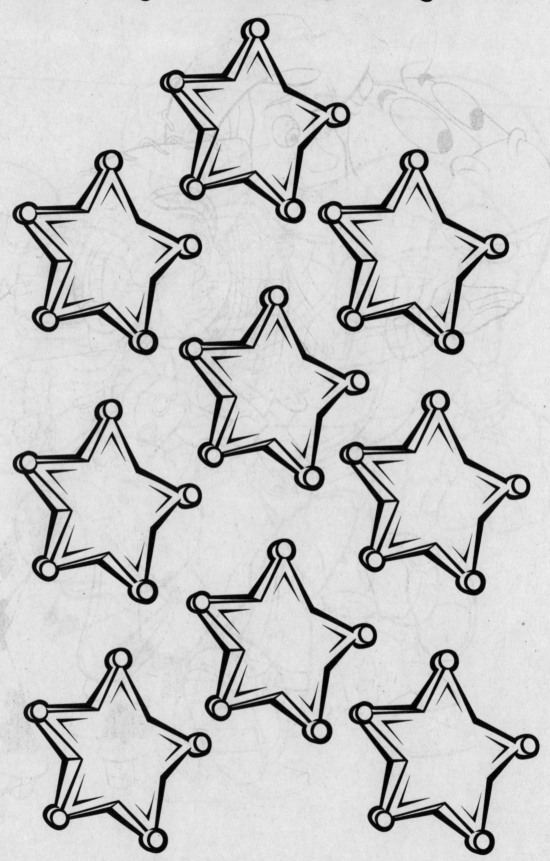

The Roundup gang is in for a surprise.

Help Woody get through the maze.

Slinky raises his coils at the Prospector.

DRAW REX!

Follow the top grid to draw Rex.

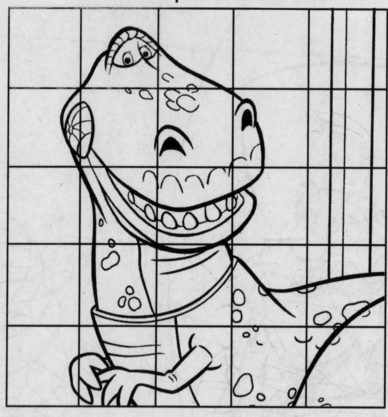

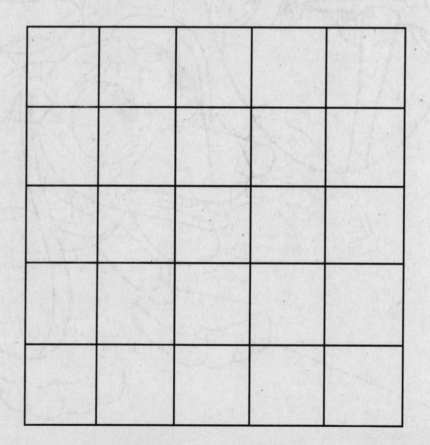

Buzz reveals his true identity!

MATCHING

Which two images are exactly the same?

A

C

B

D

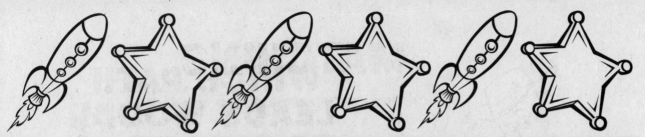

Buzz and Woody go head-to-head.

WHICH PATH LEADS WOODY TO BULLSEYE?

The Prospector blocks the way out!

SQUARES

Taking turns, connect a line from one star to another.
Whoever makes the line that completes the box puts his or her
initial in the box. The person with the most squares
at the end of the game wins!

K

Slinky stretches to help his friend.

TIC-TAC-TOE

Use these tic-tac-toe grids to challenge your family and friends!

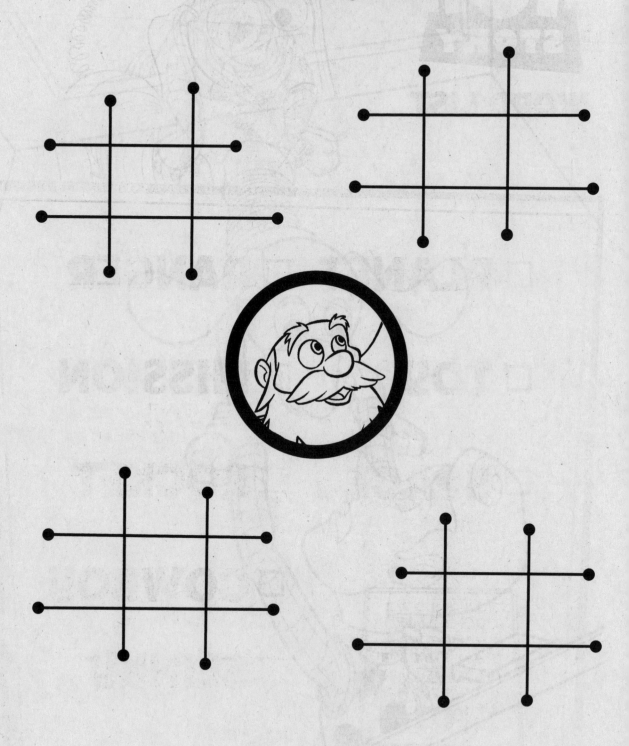

TOY STORY
WORD LIST

- ☐ **PLANET**
- ☐ **RANGER**
- ☐ **TOY**
- ☐ **MISSION**
- ☐ **SPACE**
- ☐ **ROCKET**
- ☐ **COWBOY**
- ☐ **SLINKY**

```
Z Y G S P A C E
R Y O B W O C
T X E M K M T
E Z D U L N P E
K M I S S I O N
C N B W Q L C A
O Y V H B S J L
R A N G E R M P
```

TOY STORY
WORD SEARCH

```
R A N G E R M P
O Y V H B S S J L
C N B W Q L C A
K M I S S I O N
E Z D U L N P E
T T X E M K M T
C O W B O Y R Y
Z Y G S P A C E
```

The toys give each other a boost.

THERE'S A NEW SHERIFF IN TOWN

Design and color your very own sheriff's badge!

Which way should Buzz go?

MATCHING

Which two images are exactly the same?

A

B

C

D

INTERLOCK

Using the words from the list, complete
this interlocked word puzzle.

HOWDY
SHERIFF
PARTNER
COWBOY
HERO

R

E

D

COWBOY
HOWDY
HERO
PARTNER
SHERIFF

TRANSFER

Using the paths, transfer the letters into the boxes to
unscramble the word.

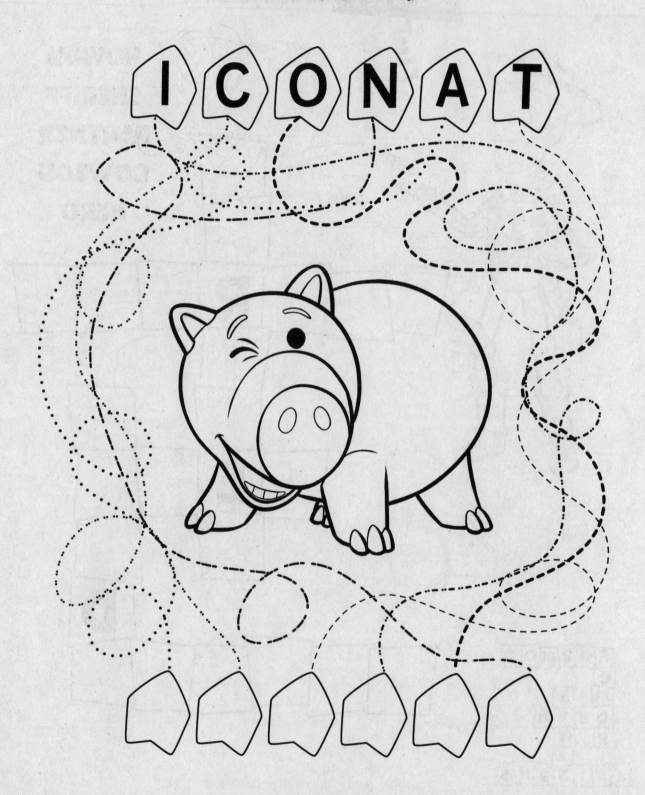

I C O N A T

Buzz, Jessie, and Woody love to play!

Rex, Hamm, and the Aliens come up with a new game.

Now Andy is all grown up.

What's going on in Andy's room? He thinks something has moved, but he's not sure what. Help him find ten things that have changed.

Woody comforts a worried Rex.

The Green Army Men give Buzz one last salute.

Andy can't take his toys with him to college.

Woody is trying to help the toys out of the garbage bag.
But something is headed their way! Connect the dots to see what it is.

The toys decide to go to Sunnyside Daycare.

Clean up Andy's room! Put the toys into the boxes by drawing a line from each toy to the correct box.

Andy's mom brings the toys to Sunnyside.

Lotso is a stuffed bear. He smells like strawberries!

The toys have arrived at Sunnyside Daycare. Look carefully at the picture for one minute. Turn the page. Draw or write down everything that was in the picture. How many things did you remember?

Use this space to draw or write down everything that was
in the picture on the previous page. How many things did you remember?

Hamm and Slinky shake all of Stretch's hands.

Jessie makes a new friend.

The Aliens find a claw!

Rex finds some dinosaurs to play with.

Woody wants to go home to Andy.

Woody soars out of Sunnyside.

Help Woody fly away from Sunnyside Daycare.

Start

Finish

TRASH

A little girl named Bonnie makes a surprising discovery.

Jessie and Buzz can't wait to play!

Here come the kids!

Help Jessie round up Andy's toys.
Circle Buzz, Woody, Hamm, 3 Aliens, Rex, Bullseye.

Slinky gets stretched *way* too far.

Meet Mr. Pricklepants!

Buttercup is a friendly unicorn.

There are some interesting things that do not belong in the daycare.
Find these eight objects that do not belong there: Andy's picture, bathtub,
flying fish, campfire, knight in armor, a chandlier, spaghetti, and a dragon.

Trixie the Triceratops is one of Bonnie's favorite toys.

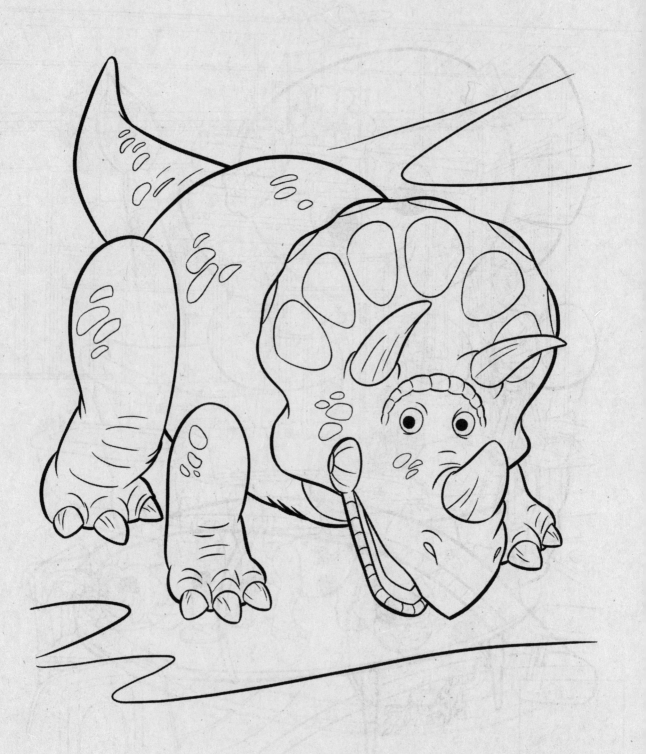

These toys are excited to meet Woody.

Jessie tries to break out of Sunnyside.

Buzz has a plan.

It's nighttime at Sunnyside but not all the toys are asleep.
Draw a line from the toy to its shadow.

The Sunnyside toys flip Buzz's switch.

Lotso is a bad bear!

Lotso has changed Buzz.

Something is wrong! Decode the message to find out what it is.

A	B	C	D	E	F	G	H	I	J	K	L	M	N	O	P	Q	R	S	T	U	V	W	X	Y	Z
1	2	3	4	5	6	7	8	9	10	11	12	13	14	15	16	17	18	19	20	21	22	23	24	25	26

23	1	20	3	8		15	21	20		6	15	18		2	21	26	26	!
																		!

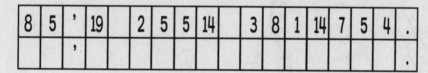

8	5	'	19		2	5	5	14		3	8	1	14	7	5	4	.
		'															.

Answer: Watch out for Buzz! He's been changed!

Buzz guards Jessie for Lotso.

Tina helps Woody use Bonnie's computer.

Buzz and Woody are sad to see Andy go—but they're happy to have a new home.

When Andy went to college, he gave his toys to Bonnie.
She loves playing with them—especially Jessie and Buzz!

Jessie the cowgirl is friendly and welcoming to every toy she meets.
She's always ready for a rip-roaring adventure.

A-MAZE-ING

Lead Woody through the maze to find Jessie.

★ ★ ★ ★ ★

START

FINISH

Bonnie makes a new friend
with big, googly eyes. She calls him Forky!

Woody welcomes Forky to Bonnie's bedroom, but Forky is confused.
He thinks the toys are trash.

SECRET MESSAGE

Cross out the word FORKY every time you see it in the box. When you reach
a letter that does not belong, write it in the squares below to reveal the secret message.

★ ★ ★ ★ ★

FORKYGFORKYEFORKY
TFORKYMFORKYEFORK
YOFORKYUFORKYTFOR
KYTFORKYAFORKYHFO
RKYEFORKYRFORKYE

Before Bonnie starts kindergarten full-time, her family takes a road trip!

Road Trip

Bonnie and her parents are going on a road trip.
Draw where you would like to take a road trip with your family.

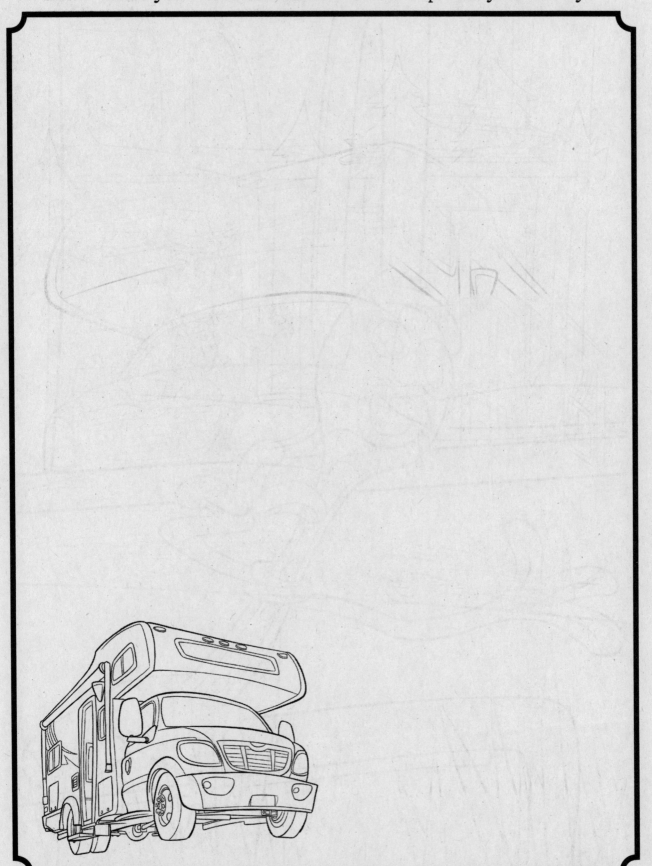

Forky doesn't want to be a toy, so he escapes out the RV window. "Freedom!" shouts Forky.

GRID DRAW

Use the small grid to help you complete
the picture of Woody and Bullseye!

★ ★ ★ ★ ★

Woody explains to Forky that he is very important to Bonnie.
The new toy can't wait to get back to his kid!

FOLLOW THE PATH

Using the pattern below, follow the correct path to find your way through the maze.

★ ★ ★ ★ ★

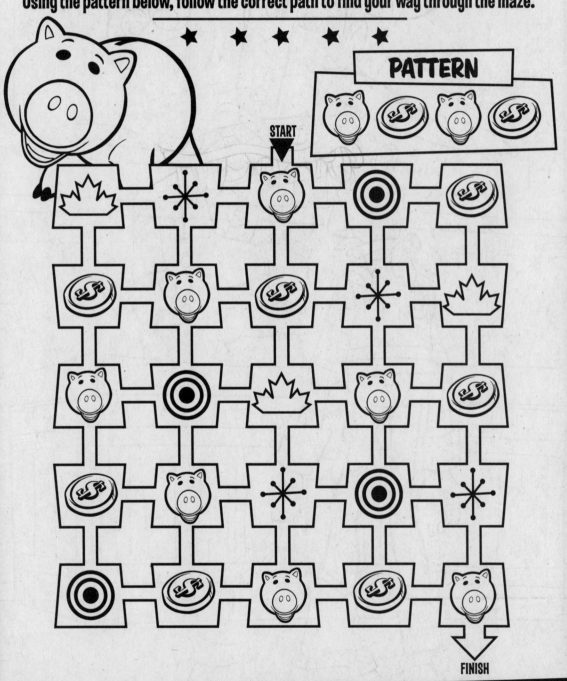

Woody recognizes that lamp. It belongs to Bo Peep! But where is Bo?

Gabby Gabby is a doll from the fifties.
She has lived in the antique store for a long time.

Connect the Dots

Woody met a new toy in the antique store.
Connect the dots to see who the toy is.

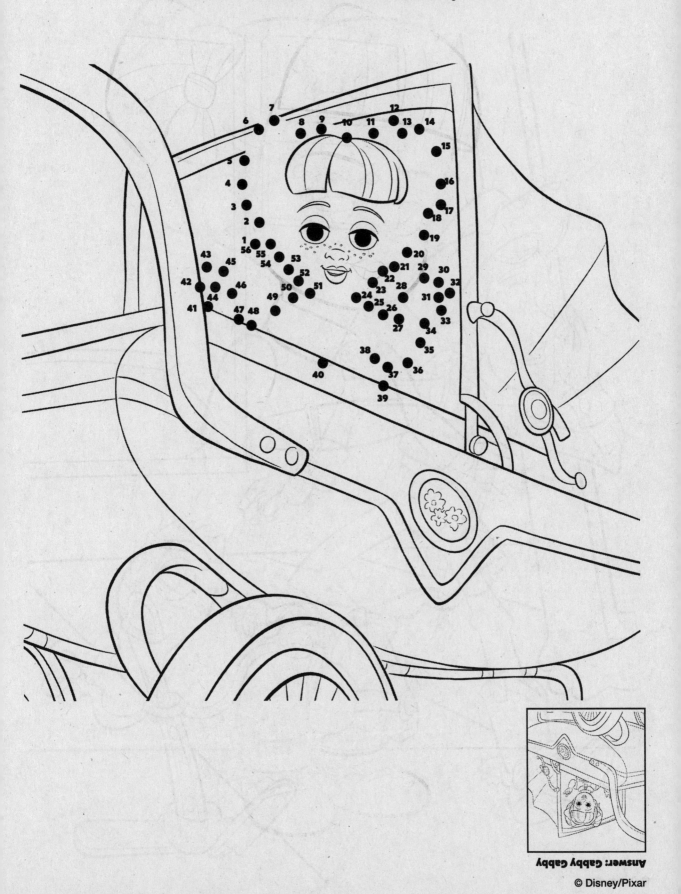

"Bo?" says Woody. Woody and Forky are looking all over the antique store for Bo.

Woody and Bo are so excited to see each other.
"I can't believe it's you!" says Bo.

MISSING PIECE

Can you find the missing piece of the puzzle?

A

B

C

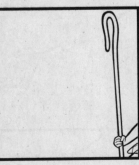

Answer: C

© Disney/Pixar

Bo escaped the antique store years ago. Now she is a lost toy.

Spot the Difference

A lot has changed since Bo lived on a lamp in Molly's room.
Can you spot the six differences between the two images?

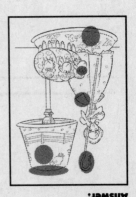

"Officer Giggle McDimples! I run Pet Patrol for Mini-opolis!"
Giggle is good friends with Bo.

COLOR BY NUMBER
Follow the color key below!

GUILTY
of cuteness!

1	2	3	4	5	6	7	8
Red	Yellow	Green	Blue	Purple	Pink	Brown	Tan

Whoosh! Buzz searches the carnival for Woody and Forky!

FINISH THE PICTURE

★ ★ ★ ★ ★

Use the example and finish the drawing of Buzz Lightyear!

Ducky and Bunny are plush toys who live at the carnival.
They want a kid of their own.

COLOR BY NUMBER

Follow the color key below!

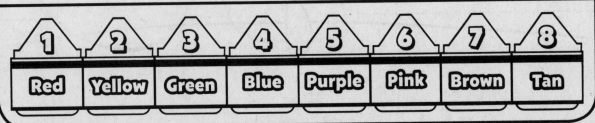

1	2	3	4	5	6	7	8
Red	Yellow	Green	Blue	Purple	Pink	Brown	Tan

Bo and her sheep stick together through thick and thin.

Lost Sheep

Billy, Goat, and Gruff are lost!
Complete the maze to help Bo find her sheep.

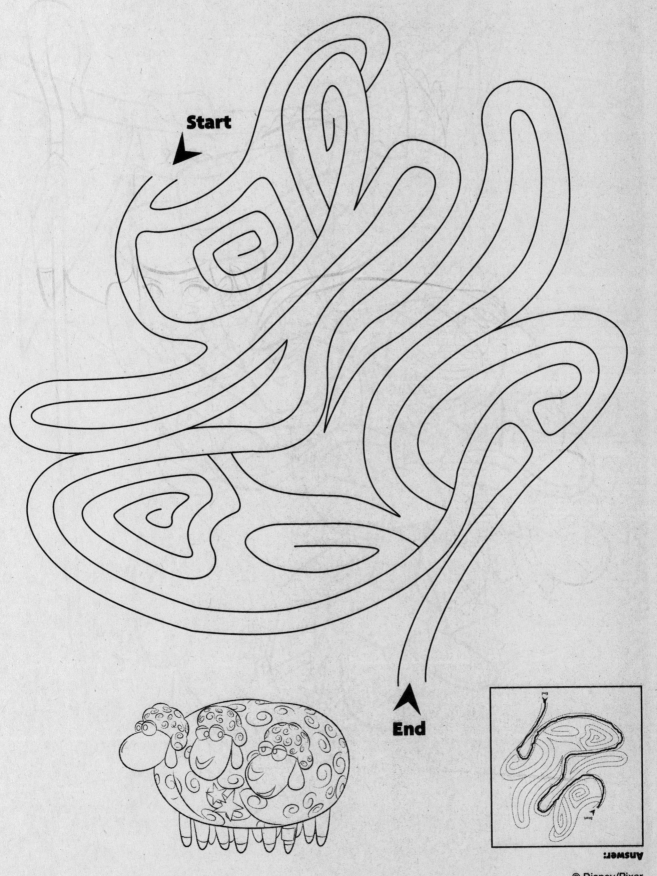

Start

End

Answer:

Woody and Forky are on their way!

COLOR BY NUMBER

Follow the color key below!

1	2	3	4	5	6	7	8
Red	Yellow	Green	Blue	Purple	Pink	Brown	Tan

© Disney/Pixar

Woody and Bo jump onto the roof of the carnival bounce house.
Next stop—the antique store!

SHADOW MATCH

Which shadow matches Bo's sheep?

★ ★ ★ ★ ★

Your Answer:

A

B

C

D

VROOM! Get ready to ride with Duke Caboom, Canada's greatest stuntman!

GRID DRAW

Use the small grid to help you complete the picture of Duke Caboom!

★ ★ ★ ★ ★

Jessie and Buzz make a great team!

Bonnie takes Forky with her everywhere she goes.

Create Your Own Toy

Bonnie made Forky out of art supplies and trash!
Draw your own new toy below.

Woody, Buzz, and Bo are always ready for adventure.